T0034988

STAR WARS™

I WISH I HAD A WOOKIEE

AND OTHER POEMS FOR OUR GALAXY

Poems by
IAN DOESCHER

Illustrations by
TIM BUDGEN

QUIRK BOOKS

PHILADELPHIA

ALSO BY IAN DOESCHER

THE WILLIAM SHAKESPEARE'S STAR WARS SERIES
William Shakespeare's Star Wars
William Shakespeare's The Empire Striketh Back
William Shakespeare's The Jedi Doth Return
William Shakespeare's The Phantom of Menace
William Shakespeare's The Clone Army Attacketh
William Shakespeare's Tragedy of the Sith's Revenge
William Shakespeare's The Force Doth Awaken
William Shakespeare's Jedi the Last
William Shakespeare's The Merry Rise of Skywalker

THE POP SHAKESPEARE SERIES
William Shakespeare's Back to the Future
William Shakespeare's Much Ado About Mean Girls
William Shakespeare's The Taming of the Clueless

William Shakespeare's Avengers: The Complete Works

TO MY CHILDREN
AND THEIR FRIENDS,

TO MY FRIENDS
AND THEIR CHILDREN.

CONTENTS

I WISH
I HAD A
WOOKIEE

A GALAXY FAR, FAR AWAY...

"Long time ago," but *when*?
"Far, far away," but *where*?
Can we go back to then?
Can we please travel there?

I WISH I HAD
A WOOKIEE

I wish I had a Wookiee,
To keep the monsters out.
If nightmares came to get me,
You'd hear Chewbacca shout.
If I were sad or frightened,
He'd come and comfort me.
A Wookiee is a kid's best friend—
At least, they ought to be.

MY PET AT-AT

Oh, if I could just get an AT-AT for a pet,
I would love him so much I would scream.
We'd take long, happy walks 'round the neighborhood blocks—
It would be every ten-year-old's dream!
We would play hide-and-seek, and so softly I'd sneak
To his cargo hold, soft as a mouse,
And our cats would run fast when they hear his big blast,
Though my mom would say, "Not in the house!"
He'd be loyal and true and be potty-trained, too,
And he'd lick me if I lost a limb.
We would cuddle at night, both wrapped up, snug and tight,
In the hangar that I'd build for him.
He would come when I call and he'd go fetch a ball,
And he'd stomp when the mailman walks by.
Oh, I'd love my sweet pet—very best AT-AT yet!—
More than all of the stars in the sky.

INGRID IS CHEWBACCA

We gathered on a Saturday—
Me, Liam, Graham, José, and Jay—
Nearby our two lightsabers lay,
And we had blasters, black and gray.
First task: decide who we'll portray!
Graham shouted, "I'll be Luke today!"
"Dibs on Han Solo!" said José.
"I'm Wedge," said Jay, without delay.
Then Liam: "Lando's mine, okay?"
I said, "I'll be Darth Vader, yay!"
Across the street, in her driveway,
Sat Ingrid, watching the display.
She came across and asked us, "Hey,
Can I play, too? What do you say?"
"That's great," I said, "Of course you may—
"We need a Leia, anyway!"

A U U U U

But Ingrid answered, with dismay,
"Chewbacca is the one I play."
I giggled, and then so did they—
Could she be Chewie? Ha, no way!
I thought she'd cry or run away,
But Ingrid wasn't led astray.
She opened up her mouth halfway—
And gave the coolest Wookiee bray:
"AUUUUUUUUUUUUUUUGHH!"
Our shock could not be kept at bay,
And we all shouted, "Yes! Hooray!"
Me, Liam, Graham, José, and Jay,
Jumped right into the *Star Wars* fray
With Ingrid, who, I can relay,
Is the best Chewie any day.

U
U
G
H
H
H

TO BE LIKE ANAKIN

I want to be like Anakin,
And podrace with the best:
I'd prove that I am brave and that
Sebulba is a pest.
I want to be like Anakin,
And fly a speedy ship:
The doomed Trade Federation falls
When I give them the slip.
I want to be like Anakin
And learn to use the Force:
I'd have a blue lightsaber that
I made myself, of course.
I want to be like Anakin,
To be a Jedi Knight:
Promoting a galactic peace
And standing for what's right.
I want to be like Anakin,
And maybe will be later:
The only thing I don't want is
To turn into Darth Vader.

STAR
WARS

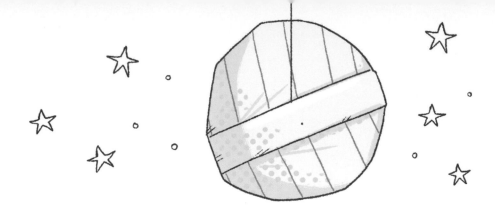

THE JAWAS TOOK MY HOMEWORK

There's an excellent reason my homework's not done,
I have been through a lot, not a bit of it fun...
I got captured by stormtroopers, one whole brigade,
To the Death Star they took me, and I was dismayed.
Soon they put me inside a detention block cell,
And I'd likely still be in that terrible shell,
Except then a sharp blast gave the Death Star a scrape—
Yes, the rebels were coming! My chance to escape!
I ran off to the hangar with all of the ships,
I jumped in a TIE fighter, my stomach did flips,
I was nervous, but wanted to flee my confinement,
And I desperately hoped to complete my assignment.
So I took the controls, though I'd not flown before,
Then I started the ship and I flew out of the door,
And of course I was heading home, straight to my work,
But then, all of a sudden, the ship gave a jerk!
A malfunction, oh no! I was going to crash—
If I wanted to live, well, then I had to dash
To the planet below, which was sandy and bleak—
I ejected just as the ship burst with a shriek.

Then I landed quite roughly on top of the sand,
As a cluster of Jawas walked by in a band.
I collapsed and they grabbed me and then, you know what?
Those small rascals took me off to Jabba the Hutt!
He demanded I pay him, but I had no money,
He got totally mad, in no way was it funny.
Next he made me his servant, to bring him his food,
Which is not all that bad when he's in a good mood.
Then, you'll never believe it—Luke Skywalker came!
In the ruckus I snuck out, and home was my aim!
So I boarded a freighter, we flew at lightspeed,
I was sure that I'd have all the time I would need.
But I miscalculated the time zones in play
Between us and that galaxy far, far away.
How upsetting—my homework was not done! Oh, dang!—
I arrived at the moment the first school bell rang.
But I'm sure you'll forgive me, since you've heard my tale—
How I battled the Empire and spent time in jail.
Pardon? What did you say about what was assigned?
It's not due till tomorrow?! Oh gosh, never mind.

STAR WARS A TO Z

A is for Anakin, from Tatooine.
B is for Bespin, the Cloud City scene.
C is for Chewie, a Wookiee who stomps.
D is for Dagobah, known for its swamps!

E is for Ewoks, more fierce than they seem.
F is for Finn, who escaped the regime.
G is for Greedo, that green guy's the worst!
H is for Han (who, with no doubt, shot first).

I's for Imperial Guards, dressed in red.
J is for Jedi, by whom peace is spread.
K is for Kessel, where spice mines are found.
L is for Leia, whose strength is profound.

     M is for Mos Eisley, where pilots roam.
     N's for Naboo, the place Jar Jar calls home.
     O is for Obi-Wan, loyal and true.
     P is for Padmé, the pride of Naboo.

Q is for Qui-Gon, who set Ani's course.
R is for Rey, who is strong in the Force.
S is for Skywalker, name so unique!
T is for TIE fighters with their loud shriek.
U is for Ugnaught, who carbonite freeze.
V is for Vader's mechanical wheeze.

     W is for Wedge, brave stand-out guy.
     X is for X-wing, which I'd like to fly.
     Y is for Yoda, the wisest of all.
     Z is for Zam Wesell, changeling oddball.

     Now, there you have it! The whole alphabet.
     Next time, I promise, I'll add Boba Fett.

COUNTING JAWAS

When I'm in bed and I can't sleep,
There is no point in counting sheep.
The only thing that does the trick
Is counting Jawas tick by tick:
One Jawa stops to say, "Good night,"
Two is a tyke of little height,
Three is one with bright yellow eyes,
Four says *"Utinni!"* (no surprise),
Five's carrying a little droid,
Six is a Jawa who's annoyed,
While seven has a tale to tell,
Eight pilots a sandcrawler well,
Nine can't help being somewhat weepy,
Ten is a Jawa . . . getting . . . s l e e p y . . .

LILY MCPHEE BELIEVES SHE IS A DROID

This is the story of Lily McPhee,
As clever a girl as there ever could be.
But one little thing makes her mother annoyed:
Seems Lily McPhee believes she is a droid.

"Around home, she's helpful with each chore and task,
She cleans and she does any favor I ask.
Her beeps and her whistles, though, I can't avoid,
For Lily McPhee believes she is a droid."

She sleeps standing up, uses only one eye,
She walks on three limbs (at least gives it a try),
She'll tell you the odds to miss an asteroid,
Since Lily McPhee believes she is a droid.

Her teacher says, "She's at the top, yes indeed!
Her math skills are perfect. I can't wait to read
Her essay about the Death Star she destroyed,
That Lily McPhee, who believes she's a droid."

She gave away all of the clothes she outgrew,
She only wears white now, with touches of blue,
She fixed up the car, made her dad overjoyed,
'Cause Lily McPhee believes she is a droid.

If you want the best friend that the galaxy's seen,
A sidekick as fast and smart as a machine,
Don't pick Molly or Oscar or Emma or Floyd,
But Lily McPhee, who believes she's a droid.

BEEP!

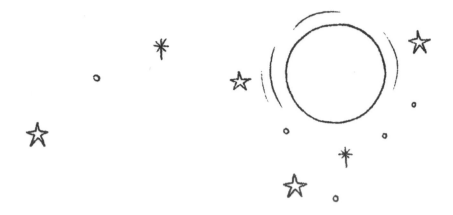

HALLOWEEN

Out this night, on Halloween,
I have counted what I've seen:
Nineteen Vaders in their robes,
Four dark gray Imperial probes,
Thirteen Leias, twenty Reys,
Forty Kylos (this year's craze),
Twenty-seven Boba Fetts,
Twelve Chewbaccas (nine were pets).
Many characters to see,
But there's only one of me.

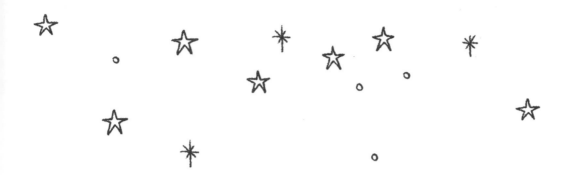

RESOURCEFUL SITH

I got my mother's lipstick,
Behind the cabinet door.
I found my father's Sharpie,
Just sitting in the drawer.
I took my sister's tape,
And knew she wouldn't mind.
I grabbed my set of shark teeth
That Grandpa helped me find.
The lipstick and the Sharpie,
I put upon my face.
I taped the teeth above it
(Used extra, just in case).
Now I'm a dreaded Sith,
The meanest of them all—
Yes, Siths are all resourceful,
Just ask me: I'm Darth Maul!

TRASH COMPACTOR

My dad yells, "Mae! What have you done?"
He bursts in with a crash.
But how can I create the scene
Unless I use real trash?

SNOW DAY ON HOTH

There was a snow day yesterday
So we all ran outside to play.
My sister was a rebel leader,
And I was Luke in my snowspeeder.
The neighbor twins were Empire troops,
Approaching us in AT-AT groups.
Augusta, from across the street,
Was Vader, blocking our retreat!
And soon our base was done at last,
Demolished by an AT-AT blast!
Augusta and the twins prevailed—
Advanced as our defenses failed!
Oh, how we shook and felt unsteady,
Until Mom yelled, "Hot chocolate's ready!"
We ran inside, escaped the weather,
Rebellion and Empire together.
We laughed about our snow day fun,
For some had lost, but all had won.

DAD'S
LUKE SKYWALKER
FIGURINE

There it was, upon the shelf,
I just couldn't stop myself.
My dad's rare, oh-so-pristine
Luke Skywalker figurine,
In the package, wrapped up tight—
Mint condition, dynamite!

But, today, I couldn't wait,
Nope, I didn't hesitate—
Ripped the plastic open fast,
Luke Skywalker, free at last.
I know what I did was wrong,
Sure enough, it wasn't long . . .

Dad walked in and saw me there,
Total silence filled the air.
I was guilty, that was plain,
I could see I'd caused him pain.
He breathed deep, got on one knee,
Then sat down and played with me.

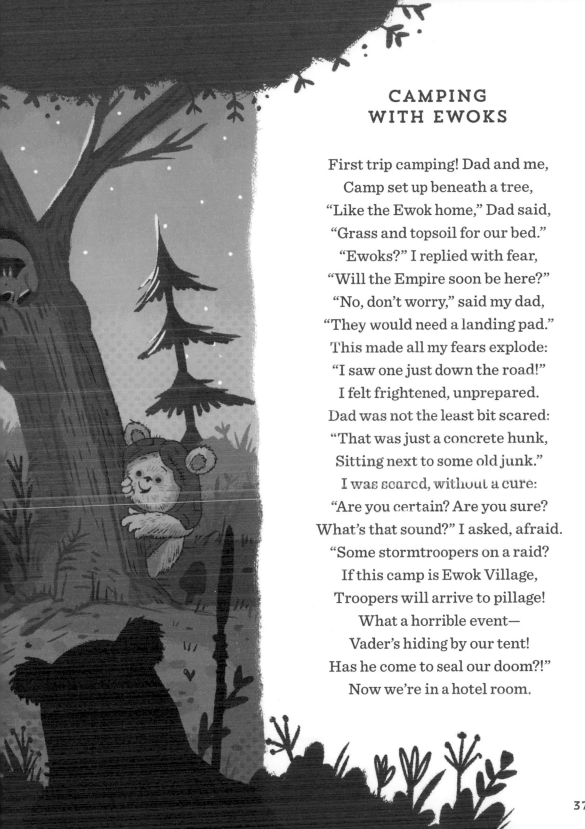

CAMPING
WITH EWOKS

First trip camping! Dad and me,
Camp set up beneath a tree,
"Like the Ewok home," Dad said,
"Grass and topsoil for our bed."
"Ewoks?" I replied with fear,
"Will the Empire soon be here?"
"No, don't worry," said my dad,
"They would need a landing pad."
This made all my fears explode:
"I saw one just down the road!"
I felt frightened, unprepared.
Dad was not the least bit scared:
"That was just a concrete hunk,
Sitting next to some old junk."
I was scared, without a cure:
"Are you certain? Are you sure?
What's that sound?" I asked, afraid.
"Some stormtroopers on a raid?
If this camp is Ewok Village,
Troopers will arrive to pillage!
What a horrible event—
Vader's hiding by our tent!
Has he come to seal our doom?!"
Now we're in a hotel room.

MOM, THE MEDIC DROID

Outside, I slipped and scraped my knee,
It bled, all filled with dirt.
I cried and yelled, Mom ran to me,
I was afraid—it hurt!
She took me in and said, with care,
"Let's fill a bacta tank!"
Soon steam was filling up the air,
Into the tub I sank.
My medic-droid-mom bandaged me,
Helped me get dressed, and then,
She said, "Luke, sir, I've fixed your knee,"
And I went out again.

LEMONADE
ON JAKKU

I'd have it made
From the cash I'd be paid
If I moved to Jakku
And I sold lemonade.

THE BEASTS INSIDE

When I am feeling sad or scared
And I would rather hide,
The acklay, reek, and nexu beasts
Are buried deep inside.
When I need their protection, they
Are quick to venture out.
They growl and snarl, they scrape their claws,
And shout their awful shout.
The acklay's voice lets out a roar
That gives me strength to speak.
The reek helps me to charge right in
When I am feeling meek.
The nexu's claws tear up my fear
When I feel cowardly.
I'm small, but I'm encouraged by
The beasts inside of me.

A GALAXY OF FAMILIES

Stan's mom and dad adopted Stan
And loved him totally,
Like Bail and Breha welcomed Leia
To their family.

Michelle was brought up by her auntie
And her uncle, too,
Like Luke Skywalker was brought up by
Owen and Beru.

Sofía grew up with her mom
And dad, both since day one.
Like Padmé, raised by her two parents
In the Naboo sun.

All families don't look the same.
What types can you think of?
The galaxy has many kinds—
Their common theme is love.

T-16 DREAMS

Khaliah feels the rush of steel
In her new T-16.
The stars and sky go rushing by
So fast, they can't be seen.
Khaliah's eyes are closed, she flies
With instinct and the Force.
The Empire trails her on her tail,
But can't set her off course.
She has the speed she knows she'll need
To get to the Alliance.
The Emperor will not deter
Khaliah's bold defiance.
Oh no! The ship begins to flip—
She feels it going down!
The T-16 begins to lean—
Khaliah gives a frown.
And then she hears, amid her fears,
Her papa's voice resound:
"Khaliah, sweet, the flight's complete,
We've landed on the ground."

THE FETTS

I bet Jango and Boba weren't totally bad,
Sometimes they must have been just a kid and his dad.
Surely Jango loved Boba, his very own clone,
While small Boba kept Jango from being alone.
Maybe they both enjoyed playing catch with a ball,
Or just jumping in piles of brown leaves in the fall,

Maybe Jango kept sweets for his son in his pockets,
Did Boba like shooting his father's wrist rockets?
Did Boba take Jango's cool ship for a run?
Yes, they must have been happy as father and son.
After all, when they're not busy planning a crime,
Even bad guys must be good guys some of the time.

NUMBERS

FN-2187 was Finn's name,
1138 the block of Leia's cell.
Bay 94 was where the *Falcon* came,
On platform 327 sat as well.

Now, if you add those numbers, you will get
Three thousand seven hundred forty-six:
Amazingly, that number is—as yet—
Exactly all the times I've seen these flicks.

FEELINGS

When I am angry at my friends
I hear the teaching Yoda sends:
"Your anger in the dark side ends"—
So I calm down, I do.

And sometimes, when I feel afraid,
I keep in mind how calm Rey stayed
When Kylo Ren made her dismayed—
Then I can do it, too.

When I get lonely late at night,
I think of Han, wrapped up all tight
Within the cold, dark carbonite—
And I know I'll pull through.

MOSQUITNOCKS

Mosquitos and mynocks are similar,
They suck on whatever they see.
While mynocks like munching on cables,
Mosquitos prefer you and me.
I'm like the *Millennium Falcon*
When mynocks were starting to snack,
I'm getting a bit irritated,
By their most unwelcome attack.
My mom starts to hand me the bug spray,
But I just give her a small shrug.
"I guess it could be worse," I tell her,
"We could be inside a space slug."

CARBONITE COVERS

June says she won't get up today,
June says she *can't* get up today.
She's far too tired,
She's uninspired,
She likes her bed.
That's why June said:
"I'm Han, wrapped tight
In carbonite."
And now she says she will not rise
Till Leia shows up in disguise.

ASTEROID FIELD

Soaring, flying, dodging, trying,
Asteroids around me,
Han got through it, I can do it,
Though the things surround me.
Odds against me, foes have fenced me
In with no escape.
One ball hits me, nearly splits me,
In this ruthless scrape.
I fly faster, I'm the master,
Swift as *Falcon* flight.
Just like Han I'll soon be gone—I'll
Win this snowball fight.

BROCCOLI NIGHT IN JABBA'S PALACE

When my mother says, "Broccoli night!"
That's when I become Jabba the Hutt.
So I grunt and I squint my eyes tight,
And pretend that my body's all gut.
Each small broccoli piece on my plate
Is a luckless Gamorrean guard.
There I sit—I'm the king of their fate—
And tonight this Hutt's heart has turned hard.
One by one, while my parents aren't looking,
I engage the trapdoor and they drop,
And the rancor below likes Mom's cooking,
For he gobbles them up where they flop.
Mom says, "You ate it all on your own!
Now, come on, tell the truth, did that hurt?"
And I grin as I sit on my throne,
While my mother serves up the dessert.

NERF HERDER

My older brother helped me with
My homework yesterday,
But he got all the answers wrong—
What will my mother say?
So, after school, I march back home,
And stomp on every stair.
Perhaps I'll get in trouble but
Right now I just don't care.
I open up his bedroom door,
My eyes are mean and grim.
"Nerf herder!" I shout, then I run.
Ha! Guess I sure showed him.

DROID HELP

My little sister's doing math
And putting up resistance.
So I act like C-3PO
To give her some assistance.
"The sum of that one's 25,
The next one's 33.
The answer to the third is clear—"
My sister laughs with glee.
She says, "Wow, you're amazing,
What a calculating whiz!
With all this help from Threepio,
I'll ace next Tuesday's quiz!"
Will Mom be pleased that I helped out
Or will she be annoyed?
My answers might be right or wrong—
Who knows? I'm not a droid.

TAUNTAUN PUPS

Kittens and puppies are cute,
But a tauntaun pup cannot be matched.
Rancors are each a big brute,
But adorable when they're first hatched.
Wampas get mean when they grow,
But a new wampa's sweeter than pears.
Wookiees are strong, as you know,
But as infants they're like teddy bears.
Babies are loved by a mother,
Even these mighty creatures as well.
And if they're like my kid brother,
They're fantastic! (Aside from the smell.)

LUKE AND ME

Luke stood near his house and watched
The suns of Tatooine—
He was dreaming of a life
Of escapades unseen.
I stand on my porch and see
The stars, which light the black.
Does Luke know, when he looks out,
That I am waving back?

CARBONITE NIGHT

When Han was in the carbonite,
What was on his mind?
Was he afraid without a light?
Scared of going blind?
Was he asleep, and did he dream?
Was it peaceful there?
Or was he wishing he could scream?
"Hey, this isn't fair!"
I don't think I'd like carbonite,
Like a frozen tomb.
So please don't tuck me in too tight,
Leave a little room!

FULLY ARMED

My smile was huge until I fell,
I gave a shout, I gave a yell—
However, much to my alarm,
I landed right on my forearm,
Then hit my head, blacked out—farewell.

I woke and caught a pleasant smell—
Nearby some flowers said, "Get well!"
A doctor came in, full of charm,
His smile was huge.

The doctor then began to tell
About my cast—my plaster shell.
Inside, they had repaired the harm
With metal plates inside my arm.
"A metal arm, like Luke? That's swell!"
My smile was huge.

POD CAR

I shut my eyes and visualize
The movement of the pod.
I start up slow, but soon I go
So fast the crowd is awed.
The competition's on a mission
But I am a survivor—
I will not yield the podrace field
To any other driver.
The gusty air blows through my hair
As I race 'round the course.
I dodge and fly, I'm guided by
The power of the Force.
I come up to the leaders, who
Are looking back at me.
Sebulba's grieving, can't believe
That I'm as fast as he.
And now I need to take the lead,
If I am gonna win.
Oh, is my skill enough, or will
Sebulba do me in?
We're near the end, just one more bend
And I will pass with ease!
My mom says, "Tough, that's long enough—
Roll up the window, please."

LOOKING FOR GUNGAN CITY

Of all the *Star Wars* characters,
Blaise liked the Gungans most.
So Blaise was thrilled when Mom and Dad
Said, "Let's go to the coast!"
The snorkel mask and air tube were
No ordinary sight,
But special underwater tools
Made for a Jedi Knight.
The sun was blazing in the sky,
The day was hot and pretty,
And Blaise swam happily for hours
To locate Gungan City.

MY ROOM'S THE *MILLENNIUM FALCON*

There are times when my mother says, "Go to your room!"
But my room's the *Millennium Falcon.*
So Chewbacca and I, we fly off with a zoom,
'Cause my room's the *Millennium Falcon.*
And it's never a punishment, I'm not annoyed,
Since my room's the *Millennium Falcon.*
We play holochess—Chewie gets beat by a droid—
In my room, the *Millennium Falcon.*
There are times we meet TIE fighters coming in fast,
'Cause my room's the *Millennium Falcon.*
But, of course, with our skills soon the danger is past,
For my room's the *Millennium Falcon.*
Then we climb in the cockpit and snuggle up tight,
Since my room's the *Millennium Falcon,*
And in less than twelve parsecs, we're down for the night
In my room, the *Millennium Falcon.*

MESSY LIGHTSABER BATTLE

"Darth Vader," I say, "it is you."
"Once again," Vader says, "it is true.
Though I should have killed you when we met,
This encounter you shall not forget."
He turns on his lightsaber, deep red,
While I turn on my blue one, with dread.
Then the battle begins! How we fight—
I dodge and I flip
And I parry and slip,
And he pushes me back
And he makes his attack,
And we're hoping the Force
Sets the other off course—
I'm a nervous but strong Jedi Knight!
When it looks like Darth Vader has won,
I remember the wise Obi-Wan,
Who said fear is a thing I must master.
But then Dad exclaims, "What a disaster!
The whole living room's been torn apart!
You will clean it all up if you're smart.
And my golf club is not a toy sword."
Now Darth Vader has fled, that Sith Lord,
But we'll soon meet again, face to face—
After I finish cleaning this place.

NABOO BATH

Brave Qui-Gon Jinn and Obi-Wan
Were in a ship with Jar Jar Binks,
Within the waters of Naboo,
Near where the colo claw fish drinks.
Their ship was slippery and wet,
It roamed along the curvy sand,
Releasing bubbles by the millions,
Every nook and cranny scanned.
Next, they approached the mighty rock
Within the darkest, deepest dregs—
A stone so massive, some believe
It's one of the sea monster's eggs.

Soon Qui-Gon had released the potion
From the planet of Chaam-peu.
The rock is covered instantly—
Protected, now, from slime and goo.
They surface near the capital,
"Our work's complete!" says Obi-Wan.
And just like that, my body's washed,
My hair is clean, my bath is done.

ON THE WAY
TO TATOOINE

Mom says that it's just a slug,
Crawling along on the ground.
Kay says it's Jabba the Hutt,
Off to his palace he's bound.
"See, Mom, the sidewalk's the sand,
Covering up Tatooine.
That stack of rocks is his fort,
There in the leaves, bright and green."
Mom looks again and she sees,
Then she says, "Look at that stick—
Is that Luke Skywalker, Kay,
Coming to rescue Han quick?"
Beaming, Kay sits on the ground,
Mom sits down, too, and they play.
Where they will go's not important—
It's what they found on the way.

CAT-AT

When my cat is stuck out
In the cold and the snow,
I pretend she's an AT-AT,
With weapons aglow.
She's sashaying her paws
With such delicate grace,
While her nose is in search
Of the veiled rebel base.
But when she comes inside
And she shakes off her fur,
She is more like a wampa,
She'll snuggle and purr.
When I kiss her, her whiskers
Are soft as a cloth,
And then we cuddle up
In our very own Hoth.

BB-8'S LOOKING GREAT

They say
a picture's worth
a thousand words—
But I say what
they say is for the birds!
To me, it seems that words are
even better—Each syllable, each line,
and every letter. And sometimes, words
themselves start to create a picture of a
thing like BB-8. Can you imagine letters
all arranged, So when you look at them
they all look changed? Perhaps some
words can give a picture birth—
Perhaps a picture's what a
word is worth!

UNDER
THE BED

A Sarlacc pit
Would barely fit
Beneath my bed,
Beneath my head.
Tonight, I heard—
It moved, it stirred—
Its tentacle
Just tried to pull
In food to feed
Its hungry need.
It's starving, see,
And it wants me.
So . . . aren't you glad
I woke you, Dad?

FINN AND POE

Finn and Poe are best of friends—
Friendship like theirs never ends.
Like them, I am on a quest
For a friend who likes me best.
If you find one, let me know—
I'm a Finn who seeks a Poe.

PRINCESS TEETH

"Go brush your teeth," said Zora's dad,
"It's almost time for bed."
"Why do I have to every night?
I hate it!" Zora said.
"But even Princess Leia had
To brush her teeth each night."
Her dad said that and Zora knew
He didn't have it right.

"Dad, Leia was a princess—duh!
That means she's royalty.
To make a princess brush her teeth
Does not show loyalty!
And also, she had Jedi strength
As Anakin's own daughter.
She used the Force to clean away
Whatever plaque had caught her."
Then Zora's dad let out a sigh,
Soon followed by another.
"You're off the hook tonight," he said,
"Just please don't tell your mother."

SALACIOUS B. CRUMB DAYS

Sundays and Mondays and Tuesdays
Are good days for having the blues days—
I feel a bit sad, just like Shmi,
And that's the most serious me.

Wednesdays and Thursdays and Fridays
Are totally up-in-the-sky days—
I'm over the hump of the week,
Like Anakin riding the reek.

Saturdays, though, are my fun days
My wild like Salacious B. Crumb days!
I'm sloppy and silly and free,
I laugh and I giggle with glee!

Saturday Crumb days are super,
But always leave me in a stupor.
They come tearing through until, then,
I'm ready for Shmi once again.

WHEN
MY BROTHER
IS MEAN,
I REMEMBER...

A Jedi Knight does not get mad,
She keeps her calm, she's not upset.
Though fighting with a Sith who's bad,
A Jedi Knight does not get mad.
And when this Padawan feels sad,
I tell myself, I won't forget:
A Jedi Knight does not get mad,
She keeps her calm, she's not upset.

AGAIN!

Episode 1 is my favorite one,
Qui-Gon is teaching a young Obi-Wan,
Keeping the Trade Federation outdone,
Also, I think Jar Jar Binks is so fun—
Let's watch it again!

Episode 2 is an awesome one, too,
Padmé and Anakin—love on Naboo!
Cloners creating a dangerous crew,
Yoda has lightsaber talents—who knew?
Let's watch it again!

Episode 3 is the best one to me:
Darkness comes over the whole galaxy,
Ani becoming a Sith by degree,
Yoda and Obi-Wan both forced to flee—
Let's watch it again!

Episode 4 shows my favorite war,
Leia shows up at the Empire's front door,
We meet Luke Skywalker, brave to the core,
Han and Chewbacca and R2 and more—
Let's watch it again!

Episode 5 makes me feel so alive,
AT-ATs attacking the sly rebel hive,
Lando's scheme when Han and Leia arrive,
Vader and Luke in a fight to survive—
Let's watch it again!

Episode 6 is the best of the flicks,
Jabba the Hutt has our friends in a fix,
Ewoks defeating scout troopers with sticks,
Palpatine crushed by his own evil tricks—
Let's watch it again!

Episode 7 can take me to heaven,
New friends and foes to meet—more than eleven!
Chewie and Han, in the *Falcon* they rev in—
Rey with her portions that instantly leaven—
Let's watch it again!

Episode 8 is amazingly great,
Rey meeting Luke to discover her fate,
Holdo and Rose are both new and first-rate,
Luke facing Kylo, who's looking irate—
Let's watch it again!

Episode 9 is an ending so fine,
Palpatine's back with a weird metal spine,
Kylo and Rey as a dyad align,
Finn, Poe, and Jannah all totally shine—
Let's watch it again!

STAR BARBER

In the *Star Wars* galaxy,
When a barber cuts your hair,
Does she use a razor with
A little lightsaber in there?

LIKE WEDGE

I don't have to be the hero,
I just want to be like Wedge—
Something greater than a zero,
Not the center, but the edge,
I would not be mean or spiteful,
I'd be loyal, that's my pledge.
Oh, my life could be delightful,
If I got to be like Wedge.

THE PREFERRED BEDTIME STORY

The bedtime story I prefer
Is not of Qui-Gon Jinn,
And how he trained a Padawan
Whose name was Anakin.
It's not the tale of Leia and
Her brother, Luke Skywalker,
And how their father was Darth Vader—
Something of a shocker!
It's not about the evil Snoke
And how he was the strongest—
The bedtime story I prefer?
Whichever one is longest.

I LIKE THE VILLAINS BEST

The good guys win, no matter what the test—
And even though this *Star Wars* fact is true,
I must admit, I like the villains best.
When Leia, Luke, and Han are getting stressed,
The three of them still manage to pull through.
The good guys win, no matter what the test!
But oh! The suit in which Darth Vader's dressed!
His red lightsaber is the coolest, too!
I must admit, I like the villains best.
I'm eager for Rey, Finn, and Poe's next quest,
To see what BB-8 will help them do—
The good guys win, no matter what the test!
The scary Leader Snoke has me impressed.
Han's son is Kylo Ren?!? I had no clue.
I must admit, I like the villains best.
Good guys are great, it's true—I won't protest.
Forgive me, then, if this seems strange to you:
The good guys win, no matter what the test—
I must admit, I like the villains best.

WHAT DID LOBOT
LISTEN TO?

What did Lobot listen to?
String quartet tunes from Naboo?
Rap or blues or jazz guitar?
Radio from Mustafar?
Rock or reggae? Jabba's band?
Luke's song (played with just one hand)?
With those headphones, bright and new—
What did Lobot listen to?

PRINCESS LEIA AND GRANDMA SHMI

It's too bad Princess Leia never knew her Grandma Shmi,
They would have been as thick as thieves, like Grandma Beth and me,
They would have had adventures on the dunes of Tatooine,
They would have done impressions of Jar Jar and Palpatine,
They would have been the best of friends within the galaxy,
If only Leia, as a girl, had known her Grandma Shmi.

BEING SICK

Breath has a noisy flow,
Voice like an alligator.
One thing is awesome, though:
I sound just like Darth Vader.

JEDI PARTY TRICKS

My parents throw a party and
They say I have to go.
I know it will be pointless if
I try and tell them no.
So I pretend each grownup can
Play Jedi tricks on me.
And I'm a trooper with a mind
That's tangled easily.
Adults say, "Wow, look how you've grown!"
And I say, "Yes, I've grown!"
They say, "You healed your broken bone?"
I say, "I healed my bone."
They tell me, "Your school must be swell."
I say, "My school is swell."
They ask, "Hey kiddo, doing well?"
I answer, "Doing well!"
They say, "Your baseball team still winning?"
And I reply, "We're winning!"
Then, when the party's over, Mom
And Dad come over, grinning:
"You were amazing! Everyone
Said you were so polite!"
They double my allowance—ha!
Now who's the Jedi Knight?

IMPERIAL MARCH

Dad always sings Darth Vader's theme
When he walks me to school.
Embarrassing in the extreme!
(But also kinda cool.)

MAY THE CAT BE WITH YOU

Cruel Kylo Ren had me confined,
He made me suffer, by the Force,
He tried to get inside my mind—
My head was pounding in due course.
The awful pressure made me scream,
My skull was sore, I filled with dread.
I woke up from the awful dream—
The cat was sleeping on my head.

FIVE-SECOND RULE

The nexu didn't care that Padmé
Tumbled to the ground—
It would have gladly munched her up,
Though dirt was all around.
So why should I refuse to eat
This muffin from the floor?
Whoever said that dropped food
Isn't tasty anymore?

RATHTAR ESCAPE!

Aboard the cargo ship Han flew,
The rathtars had escaped!
Both Rey and Finn were on the run,
They saw one and they gaped.
Chewbacca ran the other way,
To give the beasts the slip.
Han ran toward the rathtars to
Protect his cargo ship.
The rathtars were surrounding Han—
How would he ever beat 'em?
Mom says, "No playing with your meatballs—
Can't you please just eat 'em?"

STAR WARS DAY

The Fourth of May's the perfect date,
Our family's chance to celebrate.
We wake up early—we can't wait!—
And put some waffles on a plate.
My homeroom's missing this classmate!
("It's just this once," my parents state.)
The movies have begun by eight,
We watch each Episode through straight.
The pizza comes while troops create
A new Death Star to spread their hate.
My parents have a small debate:
Mom likes R2, Dad BB-8.
We finish up the movies late,
And still don't know each hero's fate.
I'm tired, so I don't hesitate—
I crawl in bed to hibernate.
My mother whispers to me, "Kate,
Dear, May the Fourth be with you!" Great!

RUBY WANTS
TO BE LIKE LEIA

Ruby wants to be like Leia:
Daring, brave, and strong,
Rather than be somebody
Who just gets pulled along.
Ruby tries it on her brother,
"No, that's not allowed!"
Ruby tries it on her dog,
"No, puppy, not so loud!"
Ruby sees how Leia stood
In front of Tarkin's face,
Proud and tough, opposing him
With wisdom, wit, and grace.
Ruby tries it on her dad,
"You said I'd get a chance!"
Ruby tries it on her mom,
"But I like wearing pants!"
Ruby loves how Leia leads
The whole Resistance crew—
Making good decisions that
Are sure to see them through.
Ruby tries it on her teammates,
"Let's go do our best!"
Ruby tries it on her friends,
"Don't argue, let it rest!"
Ruby's efforts to be more
Like Leia leave her smirking—
Ruby sees how people look
At her, and knows it's working.

MACKENZIE MCHALE, WHO WOULD NOT EAT HER KALE

Mackenzie McHale would not eat her kale,
Although her mom told her she should.
Said her Dad, "When the rebels were fighting the Empire,
They ate it whenever they could.
If you won't eat your kale, you'll turn weak and pale,
You'll turn to the dark side for good!"
And the last that was heard of Mackenzie McHale,
She'd turned into a Sith with a hood.

JOINING THE ACADEMY

Samantha Sanchez hopes that she
Can go to the Academy.
She'll learn to be a pilot true,
Fly starships of each size and hue—
With flying colors she will pass
Her courses in the X-wing class.
She'll learn to fire a blaster shot:
When to shoot first, and when to not.
She's thrilled to hear the welcome speech
From Admiral Ackbar, who will teach.
Samantha Sanchez just can't wait,
Her rebel training will be great!
She's eager to show off her tricks
At some point after she turns six.

GOOD GRIEVOUS

If General Grievous' heart
Could just increase in size,
He'd get a brand new start,
He'd see with kinder eyes.
Imagine how much fun
A droid like him could be—
With all those legs he'd run
And chuckle merrily.
He'd spin you 'round and 'round,
And never let you drop.
His joy would be profound,
His happiness nonstop.
With all those arms he'd bake
Some cookies he would share.
His fearlessness would make
Him fun at truth or dare.
If General Grievous' heart
Could just increase in size,
He'd have a better part,
Be one of the good guys.

RESISTANCE REQUIRED

Jeff has Poe-colored skin,
While Joseph's more like Finn.
Eve's skin is in between,
Like sand on Tatooine.
And BB-8's scans claim
All three are just the same:
Two eyes, one mouth, one nose,
Two arms, two legs, ten toes.
They are alike today;
Their galaxy is play.
So far they haven't learned
Why skin makes some concerned.
That lesson soon begins—
Unless Resistance wins.

SARLACC SWEETS

I'm sorry if you disapprove,
Delicious cupcake. Save your tears!
My throat's a Sarlacc pit and you've
Been sentenced to a thousand years.

HAN-ISMS

My dad giggles and snorts,
Mom cracks up and applauds,
When I say to them both,
"Never tell me the odds."

And at bedtime, Mom loves
It and she starts to glow,
When she says, "I love you,"
And I answer, "I know."

But my dad didn't laugh,
When he set out our dinner:
I said, "*One* thing's for sure—
We'll all be a lot thinner."

THE LUGGABEAST THAT
FOLLOWED ME HOME

A luggabeast came home with me today,
It showed up after school and followed me.
I wonder if it somehow lost its way,
And wound up in our far-flung galaxy.
It whimpers like it needs a place to stay,
So, Mom, I'm sure you'll understand my plea:
I promise if it makes a mess I'll sweep it,
I'll feed it every morning—may we keep it?

YODA AND PAM

Yoda speaks with mystery,
Teaching Luke about the Force,
Changing his world's history,
Setting Luke's fate on its course.

Teaching Luke about the Force,
Yoda's like my teacher, Pam.
Setting Luke's fate on its course—
Luke is young, just as I am.

Yoda's like my teacher, Pam,
Skillful, gentle, wise and kind.
Luke is young, just as I am—
With an open, willing mind.

Skillful, gentle, wise and kind,
This is what Pam hopes I'll be.
With an open, willing mind,
That is how Pam teaches me.

This is what Pam hopes I'll be:
Strong and patient, bold and wise.
That is how Pam teaches me,
Opening a young one's eyes.

Strong and patient, bold and wise,
Yoda speaks with mystery.
Opening a young one's eyes,
Changing his world's history.

VACATION PLANS

Dagobah's not a place I'd like to go—
Homes made of dirt with a roof that's too low,
Scary, dark caves with Darth Vader inside,
Dark, dreary trees where the snakes creep and hide,
Slimy, wet muck that is hard to avoid,
Monsters so big they can swallow a droid.
Let's not vacation in swamp, filth, and goo—
I'd rather go someplace nice, like Naboo.

WHAT WAS ON LUKE'S MIND?

When Luke Skywalker lived on an island, alone,
He had no one to talk to, no laptop, no phone.
Did he miss his friends Leia and Chewie and Han?
Was he tired of seafood, of cod, shrimp, and prawn?
Was he sad no one sang "Happy Birthday" to him?
After all of that thinking, when Rey climbed the rock,
Is it possible that he forgot how to talk?

IF I WERE A STORMTROOPER

If I were a stormtrooper, I'd be the best:
I'd place all the rebel scum under arrest,
I'd not hit my head as I enter the room,
I'd never give Vader a reason for gloom,
I'd practice my aim anytime there's a break
(So I wouldn't miss every shot that I make),
I'd never let Jedi trick us anymore—
I'd know that those *are* the droids I'm looking for.
So, what do you think? Tell me, what do you say?
Can I be a stormtrooper starting today?

OLD MR. JONES AND HIS
STAR WARS COLLECTION

Mr. Jones across the street
Walks like glue's stuck on his feet.
One day Pete gave me a chore:
Knock on Mr. Jones' front door,
Introduce myself, go in.
"Dare you!" Pete said, with a grin.
I crept up the Jones front walk,
Gave his door a little knock.
"Welcome, Mike," he said to me,
"Just the boy I want to see.
Come on in and visit, Mike,
I have something you will like."
There, in Mr. Jones' front room,
Pure delight began to bloom:
Scenes and starships by the ton,
Action figures, every one!
All the greatest *Star Wars* toys.
Mr. Jones and I—two boys—
Both of us were young that day.
Then I whispered, "Can we play?"
Mr. Jones smiled big and, soon,
We had played all afternoon.

A HAT FOR
KI-ADI-MUNDI

A steady hand,
Some patience, and
An awful lot of thread,
And we can knit
A hat to fit
Ki-Adi-Mundi's head.

ROLE MODEL

When Sophie saw *Star Wars* she quickly confessed,
"Mon Mothma's the character I like the best."
So Sophie approached the salon the next day,
And said, "Cut it short like Mon Mothma, okay?"
While clothes shopping, she asked her mother, Louise,
"How 'bout something white, like Mon Mothma, Mom, please?"
Young Sophie knew someday she'd grow up and lead,
Be strong like Mon Mothma, lean in and succeed.
Mon Mothma's strength, though, can't be bought off a shelf,
So Sophie determined to build that herself.

STAR WARS LUNCH

Is that a slimy sandwich,
Or one of Jabba's toads?
Is that a stale brown rice cake,
Or trash from Watto's loads?
And are these Ugnaught toes,
Or moldy carrot sticks?
Is Mom upset at me,
Or is she playing tricks?

THESE MIDI-CHLORIANS IN ME

These midi-chlorians in me,
They make me squirm in class.
These midi-chlorians, you see,
They made me drop that glass.
These midi-chlorians like pie
And now my mom is sighing.
These midi-chlorians are why
My little brother's crying.
These midi-chlorians have been
Invading me, of course.
These midi-chlorians got in
By taking me by Force.

STAR PEACE

Yes, *Star Wars* is my favorite—
Far more than dinosaurs—
I love to turn it on, and sit
And watch the rebels' wars:
The blaster shots, the Ewok fight,
The Death Star—super cool.
A Sith against a Jedi Knight,
A harsh lightsaber duel.
That galaxy's far, far away,
Where *Star Wars* never cease,
But in *my* galaxy, someday,
I'd like to see Star Peace.

WRITING THIS POEM
ON TOP OF AN ACKLAY

I'm writing this poem on top of an acklay,
Forgive me, it's hard to relax.
It seems that most acklays take quite a disliking
To poets who ride on their backs.
It's hollering loudly and trying to reach me—
It nearly got me with its claws,
And I keep on dropping my pencil when I see
How close my head is to its jaws.
Maintaining the meter is getting much harder,
I'm scrambling to finish in time.
The acklay is angry, so how can I think of
A word that will help my line end with the right sound?
Oh drat! I just fell off the back of the acklay,
I'm nervous, and filling with dread!
It's standing above me, it looks rather hungry,
I should have just stayed home instead!

INDEX

IAN DOESCHER is the *New York Times* best-selling author of the William Shakespeare's Star Wars series, the Pop Shakespeare series, and *William Shakespeare's Avengers: The Complete Works*. He has written for Marvel Comics and is a contributing author to the story collection *Star Wars: From a Certain Point of View*. He lives in Portland, Oregon, with his family. Visit him at IanDoescher.com.

TIM BUDGEN is an illustrator who can usually be found with a pencil in one hand and a sketchbook in the other. He has worked on many children's books for such clients as Scholastic, Hachette, and Simon and Schuster. He lives by the sea on Hayling Island, England, with his wife, Julia, and their pets, Baxter and Alfie.

Copyright © 2021 by Lucasfilm Ltd. & TM. All rights reserved.

All rights reserved. Except as authorized under U.S. copyright law, no part of this book may be reproduced in any form without written permission from the publisher.

Library of Congress Cataloging in Publication Data:
Doescher, Ian, author. | Budgen, Tim, 1977- illustrator.
I wish I had a Wookiee: and other poems for our galaxy /
poems by Ian Doescher; illustrations by Tim Budgen.
Summary: "A collection of kid-friendly Star Wars-themed poems"
—Provided by publisher.
LCSH: Star Wars films—Juvenile poetry. |
Outer space—Juvenile poetry. | Children's poetry, American.
PS3604.O3419 I26 2020 | DDC 811/.6—dc23
2020043936

ISBN: 978-1-59474-962-9

Printed in China
Typeset in Sentinel and Trend HM

Designed by Andie Reid
Illustrations by Tim Budgen
Production management by John J. McGurk

Quirk Books
215 Church Street
Philadelphia, PA 19106
quirkbooks.com

10 9 8 7 6 5 4 3 2 1

You've finished the book now, but please—have no fear.
There's more to enjoy on our website, my dear!
So, find a computer that's handy and near,
And visit Quirk Books to find maximum cheer!

QUIRKBOOKS.COM/IWISHIHADAWOOKIEE